DON'T VOTE FOR THE DUCK!

WRITTEN BY LAURA KENLY

ILLUSTRATED BY TANYA MANEKI

For my darling children -
may you always lead with kindness.
-L.K.

There was a huge problem
at **Washington School.**
The student in charge was a
Duck who was cruel.

The Duck hated sunshine
and he hated pie.
He wanted all flowers
to wither and die.

He built a **big wall**
around the school yard.
And said, "Vote for me
or else you are barred.

No playground for you unless you agree that the **boss** of the school should always be **me**."

"I'm in charge 'cause I'm smart," the nasty Duck said.
"There's a huge bunch of **smartness** up here in my head."

Sometimes to cause **trouble**,
he'd say things that **weren't true**.
Like, "You should eat crayons;
they're healthy for you."

The Duck despised children from **other schools**.
He said they smelled stinky and called them all fools.

He said, "**Don't come here**, you stay where you are.
I couldn't care less that you're a math star.

No one is better than the kids we have here.
At least those who **vote for me**, just to be clear."

If that wasn't enough, he said to the **girls**:
"You're only allowed to do swinging and twirls.

The rest of the playground is just for the **boys**.
And keep yourselves quiet. I don't like your noise."

But soon it was time to
have an **election**.
The Duck whined,
"Hey, I have an objection!

Why should anyone
bother to vote?
When the chance of me
losing is oh so remote.

After all I'm the **bestest**
there is, and so…"
But the students cut in and
all shouted…

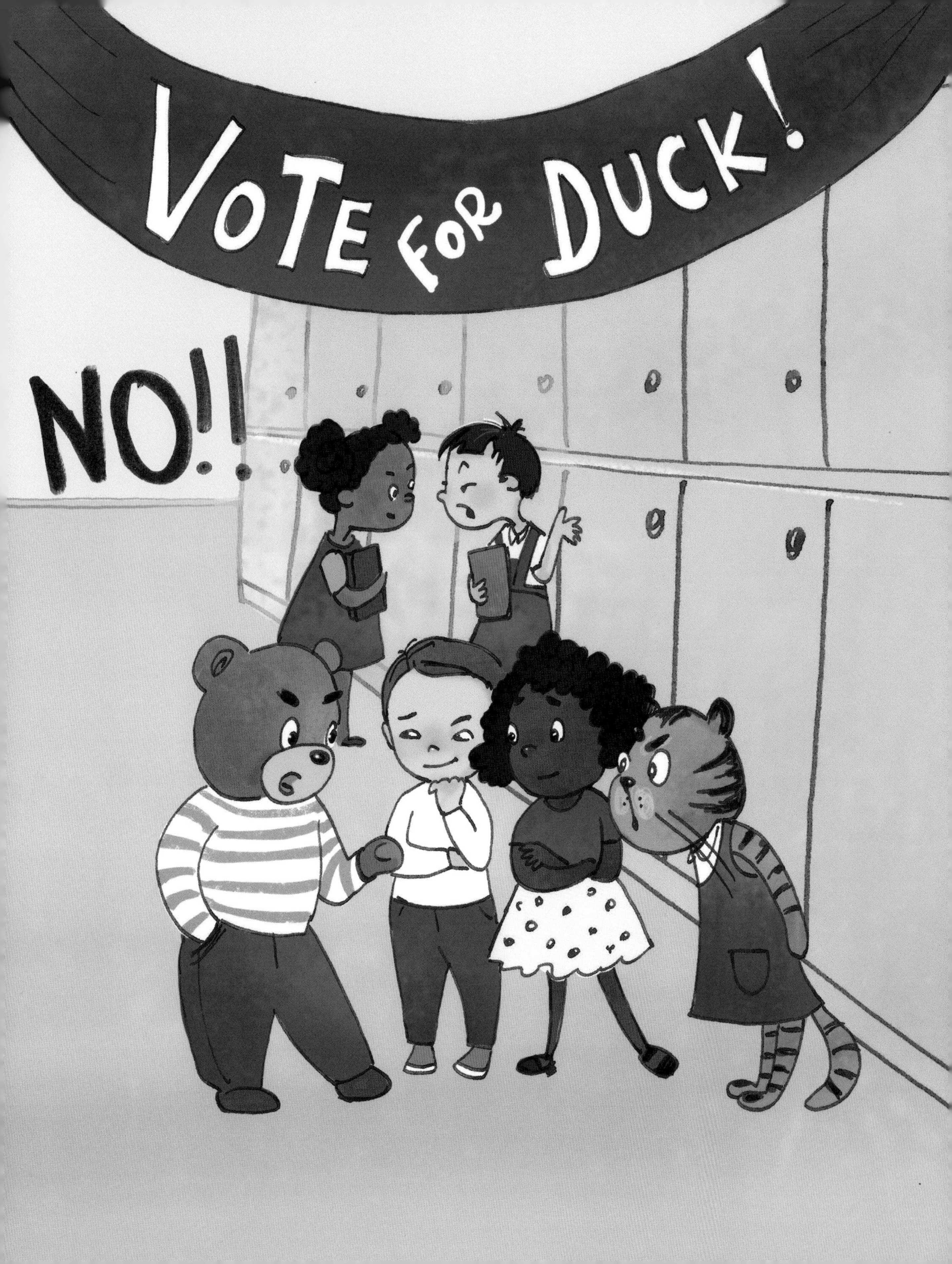
VOTE FOR DUCK!
NO!!

"When we voted last time
we had no way of knowing
How your **hatred and lies**
would just keep on growing.

But now **we know better** and we're in luck." They linked arms and shouted, **"Don't vote for the Duck!"**

"There are **smarter and kinder**
children around,
who would tear down the wall and
share the playground.

There's **Lizzy** - she's smart, she's got a good plan.
Or **Joey** - not thrilling, but does what he can."

"There's **Bernie** who always recycles his trash.

There's **Mikey**
who's willing to give out
his cash."

They had lots of choices and were quickly struck
that they'd **all** do a better job than the Duck!

"Hurray! We can do it! The Duck's time is done.
We must **join together** and stand up as one.

We'll stop at nothing and go to the polls.
Each single vote counts to achieve all our goals."

"The school will get better, we won't stay this stuck.
If we unite and
DON'T VOTE FOR THE DUCK!"

Author - Laura Kenly

Laura Kenly is an American living in London and
mother to three tough critics:

"This book is really good but it would be better if there
were unicorns or mermaids in it."
- K, age 5

"How come you don't say anything about how dangerous
it is when the duck is standing on the wall? You'd be screaming
if that were me."
- J, age 7

"Ducks don't wear hats."
- B, age 2

Illustrator - Tanya Maneki

Tanya Maneki is an illustrator from Ukraine. She started drawing
at an early age and studied art at the School of Fine Arts. After
high school, she continued her education at the Art Academy.
Now Tanya works as an independent artist with authors from all
around the world. Books with her illustrations have been published
in the US, UK, Australia, Europe, and Asia.

Printed in Great Britain
by Amazon